Robbie's World

And His SPECTRUM of Adventures!

Book 2

Chapters 5-8

Story and Illustrations by
Cindy Gelormini (Robbie's Mama)

Xulon Press

Xulon Press
2301 Lucien Way #415
Maitland, FL 32751
407.339.4217
www.xulonpress.com

© 2020 by Cindy Gelormini

Printed in the United States of America.

Paperback ISBN-13: 978-1-6322-1849-0
Hardcover ISBN-13: 978-1-6322-1850-6
Ebook ISBN-13: 978-1-6322-1851-3

Dedicated to: All my Bubbas

Robbie is a penguin who loves riding in the car.

His Mama always says, "I love you just the way you are."

Chapter 5

Twirling Bows and Bedtime Woes

Robbie is now **5** years old and as his body grows
he's full of so much energy,
where it comes from no one knows!

He likes to hop and jump and
spin and walks up on his toes,
and plays a silly game of spinning
all his sisters' bows!

"Mom!" his sister Dede yelled, "He's being such a pest!
He's twirling all my hair bows and
he's making them a mess!
I have to go to school now and I need one to get dressed!"
"Don't worry," Mama said, "I have one hidden in a chest".

Dede wore a purple bow and Lulu always pink.
Mama fixed their feathers,
"Now it's perfect! Don't you think?"

"Put your coats on." Mama said,
"Let's all get in the car."
Then while dropping them
at school said,

"I love you just the way you are."

9

Next was Robbie's turn to go get dressed and
catch the bus. He had a whole routine.
If it got messed he'd make a fuss!
Mama fed and dressed him,
but his bus was running late.
Robbie started to undress
because he didn't
like to wait!

10

When Mama came back in the room
his clothes were on the floor!
She quickly got him dressed again
and rushed him out the door.
Mama learned to schedule
every minute on the clock,
or Robbie got his point across,
even though he couldn't talk!

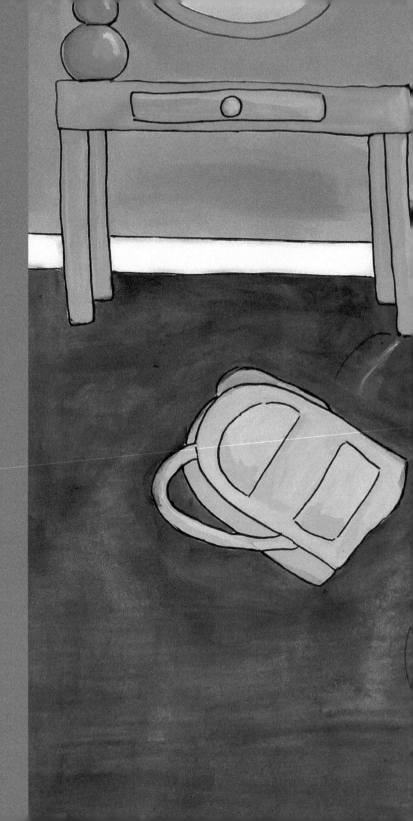

As soon as Robbie
got home at
the end of every day
he'd run into the house
and take his clothes off
right away!

He'd find his sisters' bows,
and then he'd jump and
laugh and spin,
and watch his favorite
TV show
over and over again.

At dinner time
the whole family
would sit down at the table.
But Robbie hated
sitting there.
It's like
he wasn't able.
Mama used to try so hard
to make him sit and eat,
but he'd scream
and cry and bite, then
throw himself down
at her feet.

Finally she gave in
so they all could eat in peace,
and let him eat the way he wants
in front of the TV.
Mama learned to pick her battles.
Some weren't worth the fight.
Sometimes she had to just give in
to have a peaceful night!

17

One Sunday they had dinner with
Aunt Ann and Uncle Tony,
who said, "What's wrong with him?
Why won't he eat his macaroni?"
"He doesn't like the texture."
Mama said, collecting dishes.
"He won't eat anything too soft
or anything that squishes."

Night time came and Mama said,
"It's time to all go sleepies!"
Getting Robbie's sisters off to bed
was always easy.

20

Mama kissed and tucked them in,
"Goodnight Lulu and DeDe."
It didn't take them long to fall asleep
and both start dreaming.

Then she'd try with Robbie saying,
"Let's go brush your teeth."
She tried the best she could
to keep him on a bed routine.

But Robbie still was wide awake,
jumping up and down,
so Papa gave him medicine
each night to wind him down.

Finally at midnight
he calmed down and then he yawned.
Mama tucked him in
hoping he'd sleep at least 'til dawn.

She used a weighted blanket
that would help to keep him calm.
She shut the lights and locked
the doors and then set the alarm.

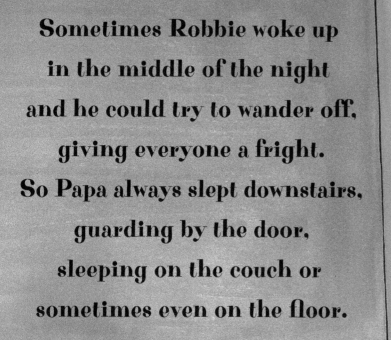

Sometimes Robbie woke up
in the middle of the night
and he could try to wander off,
giving everyone a fright.
So Papa always slept downstairs,
guarding by the door,
sleeping on the couch or
sometimes even on the floor.

Sometimes he got up at 3 A.M., wide awake.
Papa'd make sure Robbie didn't have a tummy ache.
The only thing that calmed him down
was watching TV shows, so Papa stayed right by him
on the couch where he could doze.

Tonight though Mama checked on him and
he was fast asleep, so quietly she kissed him seven times
upon his cheek.

She looked out of the window at the moon and at the stars.

Then she said, "Goodnight my love,

*I love you just
the way you are."*

Mom's Minute

This story is all about "stimming". Autistic kids love to "stim". This can be in the form of hand flapping, jumping, twirling, spinning, rocking, or making vocalizations. When Robbie was two he started grinding his teeth and squeezing his hands. By the time he was 5 years old he was a bundle of energy. He always squinted to look at things through one eye. He jumped all the time, flittered his fingers in front of his face, made loud vocalizations when he was excited, laughed for no apparent reason, and he would grind his teeth so much that he ground his baby teeth down to nothing. Autistic kids seem to need to stim when they are excited and happy, or also when they are upset, agitated, or on sensory overload. It seems to calm them down when they're upset, but it also feels good when they're really happy. In school they make kids keep their stimming under control, but when they get home they seem to need stim to release all of their pent up energy.

On days when he was exceptionally hyper, Robbie would stay up until midnight. On other days, if he fell asleep early, he would wake up at 3:00 AM, just like in this story. He would be wide awake, and would want to watch his TV, and would jump up and down making plenty of noise. Since he had the habit of eloping, my husband really did sleep in the living room near the front door, and even sometimes slept on the floor. Sometimes he could get Robbie to lay down with him in the middle of the night and "camp out" on the floor and go back to sleep.

When he was five years old we finally called the Developmental Pediatrician who diagnosed his Autism and he prescribed Clonidine, a blood pressure medication, to slow Robbie down on nights when he wouldn't go to sleep. He eventually ended up taking this medication every single night for the rest of his life.

One of Robbie's favorite stims was grabbing a pair of shoes and twirling them around and around. But this would end up tying the shoes up in knots. His sisters used to get upset because then they couldn't put their shoes on! So I gave him an old pair of shoes and designated them as his "flingers" to stim with when he got home from school. Since penguins don't wear shoes in the story, I substituted hair bows. :)

Robbie always refused to eat at the table. It was a real battle. He would kick, scream, pinch, bite, and throw himself on the floor. Eventually I just gave in and let him eat in his room in front of the TV. His school was able to teach him to eat at the table and it seemed so easy for his teachers to teach him! I always felt guilty about this and felt like I had failed as a parent for not following through and really working on this skill. In hind sight I guess it was not such a big deal, because as he grew up he eventually ate at the table. I mention this for other parents to help them let go of the parental guilt. Sometimes we have to let things go and just do the best we can.

On this vacation to the beach Robbie was stimming constantly. You can see in the photos he is squinting his eyes. His sister took away the shoes that he was "flinging" to take a photo. When we tried to take a picture in front of the lighthouse, we tried to make him stop stimming and he had a tantrum.

Here is a photo of Robbie eating a snack in front of the TV. He took over his sister's bedroom watching their TV, so eventually we had to switch all of the rooms around. We turned this bedroom into Robbie's own TV room.

Chapter 6

Bus Chase and Thanksgiving Shakey Shakes

Mama loved the Autumn and
the color of the leaves.
She loved the red and orange and
the yellow on the trees.
She really liked the weather
as it started to get cool.
Robbie loved it too because
he loved to go to school.

Every morning Mama would put Robbie on the bus.
Sometimes they'd run late, and
drivers got mad and would fuss.
Mama held his flipper as they walked out to the street.
He didn't understand that there were dangers
he could meet.

Miss Nina turned on flashing lights,

and even a stop sign.

But sometimes drivers never stopped

and even drove right by!

Mama would get worried

that a car would hit her son.

She shook her flipper

and she yelled,

"Hey! Stop everyone!"

One day, a driver drove right past
the bus and flew on by.
He didn't even see the flashing lights,
or red stop sign!

Mama kicked her slippers off and
ran right down the block.
She banged upon his window and said,
"Hey! Next time you stop!"

Mama went inside and then
she called up the police.

"No one's stopping for the bus.
They're flying down the street!

Maybe we could put a sign
that says,

'Child with Autism.' "

He said, "We can't
do that just yet.

But we will surely
help him."

The next day Mama woke up
and she went downstairs to eat.
She looked out of the window and
she looked across the street.
There was a policeman watching traffic
from his car like Robbie's guardian angel,
sitting watch and standing guard!

44

Mama felt much safer
walking Robbie to the bus.

She waved to the policeman and said,
"Thanks for watching us!"

Every day they watched to see
if cars would go or stop,
and if they passed the bus
they got a ticket on the spot!

45

Late November came and all the leaves fell off the trees.
Thanksgiving Day had come and Mama
knew what that would mean,
Robbie may get moody, he may even cause a scene.
Holidays upset him, they messed up his whole routine.

Papa went to football, watching Robbie's sisters cheer.
Mama stayed with Robbie, like she did year after year.
So Mama set the table, then she went to check the turkey,
while Robbie twirled his sisters' bows
and watched his favorite movie.

47

His family never went together,
anywhere at all.
If Robbie had to go with them,
he'd scream and yell, then fall.

So one would always stay home
while the other drove them all.
Mama went to ballet.
Papa took them to softball.

They DID try taking
Robbie once to
watch his sisters' game.

They lasted only
five minutes
before he ran away!

Today the family came for dinner,
Uncle Tony and Aunt Ann.
Robbie sat for five minutes,
then he got up and ran.

Robbie ate some turkey, but
he would not eat green beans.
He never ate his veggies,
nor anything that's green.
He didn't eat wet mushy things,
he'd spit them out and scream.
But changed the rules
with two wet things,
chocolate pudding
and ice cream!

As day turned into night,
Robbie's mood changed so it seemed.
He kept running back and forth
and it appeared that he was steamed.
To him the day was over, time for all to go to sleep.
He started throwing cushions,
slamming doors,
so they would leave!

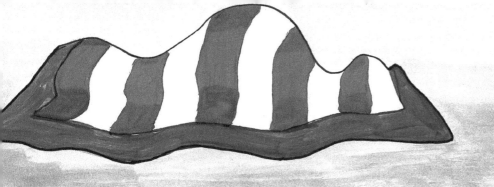

He hid under a blanket in his room to hide away.

This was too much for him to handle,

this had been a stressful day.

Then he started moaning, 'cuz he had a tummy ache.

Then Papa had to hold him as he got the shaky shakes.

Mama stayed up all night
just in case he needed help.

When he woke up in the morning
he was his perfect penguin self.

Mama called the Doctor and he said to bring him in.

He said he thought that it was time to see a specialist.

She drove him to the hospital. They did some special tests.

They met a very nice Nurse and nice Neurologist.

They tried to talk to Robbie. Mama said he couldn't speak.

Then they prescribed some medicine and said, "Come back next week."

Mama understood
that this was only just the start.
He'd get the shaky shakes again
and boy this will be hard.

Mama held his flipper
as they walked out to the car,
and had a talk with God
about the boy who stole her heart.

"How am I going to do this?
This is going to be too hard."

Then she heard a little voice
speaking from deep inside her heart.
"You're not alone, I'm with you.

I am never, ever far,
and I love Robbie even more
than you do in your heart.

From the first day that you prayed,
what did I tell you from the start?
To daily tell your son,

I love you just the way you are!"

Mama picked up Robbie and she squeezed
him really hard.
And YOU know what she said
as she put Robbie
in the car...

Mom's Minute

The bus chase in this story really happened! Every morning it seemed a driver would pass the bus and it got really frustrating. I contemplated keeping an egg in my pocket to throw at oblivious drivers. Finally one day I did kick off my slippers and ran after a car and banged on his window! He never noticed the flashing red lights on the bus or the stop sign. I called the police to request a sign, but at the time, for some reason, they couldn't get me one. But they DID send a police officer to sit across the street and watch for drivers. They gave quite a few tickets! The laws are different in each state, but typically drivers must stop 10 feet away on both sides of the street when a school bus stops and puts out a stop sign. If not, they will get a ticket and have to pay a fine and get points on their license. Autistic kids have no fear of danger so they are especially at risk of running away in front of the bus. **Parents, you will need to be your child's advocate in many situations in their lives!**

Due to Robbie's tantrums and running away whenever we went out in public, it eventually became nearly impossible to take him anywhere. We did split up all of the activities and one of us always stayed home with Robbie. Sometimes I wondered if other families thought we were divorced because my husband and I were never together at the girls' activities. As Robbie got older though, his school took him on outings to the community to teach the students how to become comfortable with going out in public. After a while, when he became a teenager, we were able to take him places. But there was a good ten year period that we could not go anywhere.

Robbie really hated holidays because it threw off his routine and he did throw pillows and run back and forth whenever he was agitated. Over the years, these times off of school got worse and worse, and he began to vomit on the holidays. When he was 17 he had his first seizure. Then he began to get sick on every holiday!

Seizures can be brought on by stress, so we began to really play down holidays and tried to keep Robbie as calm and happy as possible on those days. A lot of patience, compassion, love and prayers were the only way to get through it!

When he was little I had to put Robbie on a harness (like a child leash). I got a lot of looks from other people, but I didn't care. It was either that or lose him and have to call the police! When he got older though he finally stopped running away!

Denise (Dee Dee) And Patti (LuLu) Cheering at a football game.

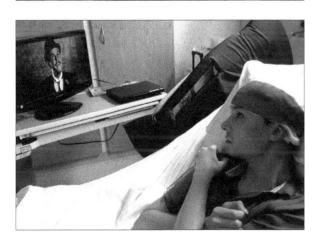

Robbie getting an EEG in the hospital. He had to stay in bed overnight. He loved watching Mary Poppins, especially the scene with the dancing penguins! By the next morning he ripped all the wires off, so it was time to go home!

Chapter 7

Christmas Day and
A Jolly Runaway

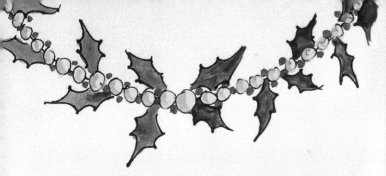

In the first week of December
Mama started to make plans,
for Christmas time was here,
but Robbie just was not a fan.

His sisters were excited,
and couldn't wait
to trim the tree.

But Robbie didn't like that
holidays wrecked his routine.

Mama packed them up one day
and took them to the mall.
She tried to get a picture of them all
with Santa Clause.

Robbie really hated waiting in a big, long line.
He plopped himself right on the floor
and he began to whine.

Mama grabbed her phone
and played a video for him.
Then immediately he calmed down,
and he began to grin.

Mama turned and she began to chat with other moms, then turned and looked toward Robbie, but

Oh NO! Her boy was gone!

"Robbie, Robbie!" she called out,
and she looked all around.

So many people in the mall,
how would her boy be found?

She ran to find security and told them he was lost.

She gave them his description and explained he couldn't talk.

They checked on all their cameras
and they made the doors all lock.
They made a big announcement and
they turned the music off.
"No one's going out, because now all the doors are locked,
until we find
the little penguin boy
who has been lost!"

Mama grabbed ahold of Robbie's sisters and
she prayed to send his guardian angel
to protect her boy who strayed. She asked to Lord
to please return her penguin safe and sound.

Then suddenly she heard
someone shout out,

**"He has
been
found!"**

Mama wiped her tears away and
then she turned around.
"Robbie please stop doing this,
you're stressing Mama out!"

75

"I guess we're going to leave now,

there's no way we're going to stay.

You win!" Mama said to him, "I guess you got your way."

As they were walking out they heard a voice say, "Ho Ho Ho!

Is this the little penguin who has put on quite a show?"

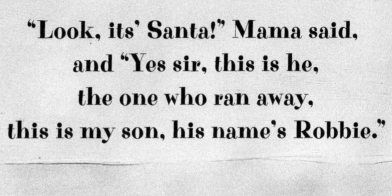

"Look, its' Santa!" Mama said,
and "Yes sir, this is he,
the one who ran away,
this is my son, his name's Robbie."

Santa posed for pictures
and Robbie giggled at his beard.
Santa took their lists and said,
"Merry Christmas, Happy New Year!"

Everyone was happy now
and walked out to the car.
Mama said to all,

*"I love you
just the way you are."*

Two weeks later Robbie had a concert at his school.
Some kids sang "Jingle Bell Rock",
wearing glasses to look cool.

Some kids did a line dance wearing
green and red and yellow.
Others sang of reindeer and about a jolly fellow!

One boy played the piano and he sang all by himself.
The music teacher looked so cute,
he dressed up like an elf!

No one in Robbie's class could sing.

They all needed more help.

So his teacher got creative and they all shook jingle bells!

Christmas morning came and
it was time to open gifts.

Would Robbie wake up happy?
Through the day would his mood shift?

Everybody woke up and
the girls ran down the stairs.

When they saw the gifts they yelled out,

"Santa Clause was here!"

Papa started handing out
the gifts under the tree.
Robbie wasn't interested,
he'd rather watch TV.

His sisters squealed out
in delight and
opened up their dollies,
while Mama wrestled Robbie
in between her sips of coffee.

Mama helped him open gifts, flipper over flipper.
His Grandma sent him a new coat with
buttons and a zipper.

Santa gave him a toy car that sounded like "ZOOM ZOOM!"

Robbie didn't like it so he threw it across the room!

"Hey!" said Mama, "That's not nice!

Robbie, don't do that!"

Robbie thought that this was funny,
so he began to laugh and laugh!

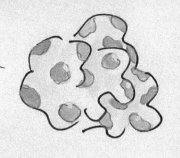

So every present after that he tried to throw again.
Mama quickly caught on and said,
"Throw paper instead!"
Everybody joined in and they crumpled up the paper,
then threw it across the room, and
Mama cleaned it all up later.
Now it's a tradition. Robbie does it every year.
He throws the paper, then he laughs,
and smiles from ear to ear.

89

After their last holiday when Robbie got upset,
they knew their lives were different now,
it's useless just to fret.

They learned to do things Robbie's way,
each and every minute.

They laughed and said,

"It's Robbie's world,

and we just all live in it!"

They made it through the day
with family visiting in shifts.
They ate a little bite,
and quickly opened
up the gifts.

Everybody made sure Robbie wouldn't end up sick.

They went home earlier this time.

They learned that was the trick.

Robbie took a bath and he put on his brand new jammies.

His Papa and his Mama just were happy he was happy.

They tucked him in that night and left his door a bit ajar.
They gave him kisses and they said,

"We love you just the way you are."

Mom's Minute

Robbie didn't enjoy Christmas because he didn't understand why his routine was changed. He also didn't like opening gifts because it seemed like a task that was work to him. He didn't even enjoy toys because he didn't understand how to play with them. Eventually we just started to give him food as gifts, treats that he enjoyed like popcorn or cookies, and he did enjoy opening that. We had to make the gift opening time pretty quick because he had a very short attention span. And oh yes, he always threw his gifts across the room! So we eventually made sure his gifts were soft items that wouldn't cause damage when they were thrown!

As for the story of running away at the mall, that actually happened to my baby brother when I was 14 and I never forgot the feeling of the entire mall going on lockdown, and fearing that someone had stolen my little brother! So If I ever took Robbie out somewhere I made sure he was sitting in a stroller or a shopping cart, contained so he couldn't get away. When he grew too large for a stroller I never took him to the mall. He did run away from me in a fabric store once and they locked down the store. We found him hiding behind a roll of fabric, and of course he thought it was hilarious. After that, I just stopped taking him out to stores all together and only shopped while he was at school, or left him home with his father.

In this story Mama says "You're stressing Mama out!" and that's no joke! At this point, you should be getting the idea that life is quite a dramatic roller coaster ride living with a child with Autism, and you never know what to expect. It can be very stressful for parents. If you want to know how to help out parents, they can use help with baby sitting or just an extra set of hands. Especially if they are a single parent, they may need help to just be able to go to the grocery store!

Spectrum: In the part of the story where they are doing the holiday program at school, you'll see the varying degrees of what students are capable of doing. Some can dance and understand instructions, but are not verbal. Some are high functioning and can sing, and even play the piano. But Robbie's class is very low functioning. No one in his class can talk or sing and can barely understand basic commands. The purpose of this part of the story is to show the spectrum of abilities. Some people with Autism are high functioning (Usually called Asperger's Syndrome) and you can barely tell that they have Autism. They usually have difficulty socializing and may have a few behaviors, but you can carry on a full conversation with them. At the bottom of the spectrum would be someone like Robbie who was completely non-verbal, did not really understand speech, wore a diaper into adulthood, and only functioned on the mental level of a toddler. Others with Autism can fall anywhere in between. They are all very different individuals and the best way to relate to them is simply to get to know each person individually.

Meet the cast of characters! From left to right: Robbie's Gram, (Aunt Rosie was her sister.) and his Aunt and Uncle. Standing behind Patti (Lulu) is her husband Brendan. Then comes Robbie, the center of attention always! Behind Robbie is "Baby" David who is now 6'4" tall. Next is Denise (DeDe) and her husband Chris. Furthest to the right is me and my husband Robert. Robbie of course refused to wear a hat and is wearing the Scrooge T-Shirt because he hates holidays. Although, if he gets to spend the day with his sisters, he's happy. And when Robbie's happy, we're ALL happy!

Chapter 8

Winter Break on a Snowy Day

The morning after Christmas Robbie woke up really fast!

He thought the bus was coming and his routine was back on track.

His sisters didn't wake up and his Mama was in the bath.

"Oh No! What's going on?!"

he thought, and gave his head a smack!

101

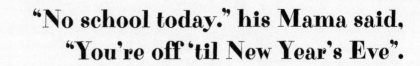

"No school today." his Mama said,
"You're off 'til New Year's Eve".

She had no plans and wished that she
had something up her sleeve.

She'd tried to take him out
but he threw tantrums in the stores.

Yet, if they stayed at home
he'd have a fit 'cuz he was bored.

He always watched the same old thing, his Dolphin Land cartoons.

His Mama tried to give him something else but he refused.

He made her change the movies for him every couple minutes, until she lost her patience.

"That's enough! I just can't take it!"

Usually on weekends
Robbie went to swimming lessons.

The pool was just his favorite place,
for him it was just heaven.

But everything was always closed
throughout the Christmas break.

Mama had to find some ways
to fill up all the days.

She bundled up the girls and
put their hats upon their heads.
She buckled Robbie in the car and
went out to the shed.
Then she came out carrying
two saucers and a sled.

Lulu said to Deedee,
"I get the one that's red!"

107

She drove them to a parking lot that had a great big hill.
They couldn't wait to get out.
The girls were just so thrilled!

Robbie took his hat off and his boots inside the car.
"Where are your boots?" asked Mama.
"I've no idea where they are!"

Dede grabbed her saucer and
her sister grabbed hers too.
"Who's ready for a push?"
"I am!"
"Here you go Lulu!"
Dede started whining and she said,
"Me too! Me too!"
Mama pushed her down the hill.
She squealed and yelled,

"Woo Hoo!"

"OK Robbie, it's your turn!"
Then she found his hat.
She put it on his head and
made a face so he would laugh.
Then she put his hood on
and she tied it with a bow,
then his mittens and
his boots, to keep his feet
warm in the snow.

She put him on the sled and showed
him where his feet should go.
Then she sat behind him
and said,

"OK, here we go!"

They slid right down
the slippery hill
and wow!
It went so fast!

He thought that
it was funny!
Robbie giggled and
he laughed!

When they got down

to the bottom,

they didn't stop!

They crashed!

Then everybody fell

and then they laughed,

and **laughed** and **laughed!**

Robbie's mittens flew off

and his hat came off his head,

then his flippers got too cold,

and he was starting to get wet.

Then Dede started crying, because snow got in her boots.
Then her sister started whining,
"Now what's wrong with you Lulu?"
Lulu's flippers got so cold, that they began to sting.

First she started crying,
and then she began
to scream.

Mama packed up everyone
and pulled them up the hill.
"That's ENOUGH fun
for today," she said.
"Mama's had her fill".

Finally at home they took off
all of their wet clothes.
Mama dried their mittens
and she put them near the stove.
Mama warmed them up, her breath was hot,
it felt like steam. "I know" Mama said,
"Who wants hot cocoa
with whipped cream?!"

First she gave
them baths
so they could
all warm up
their toes.
Then she wrapped
them each in towels
and then she kissed
them on the nose.

They all put on their PJ's, then their soft and fuzzy robes.
Then Mama gave them marshmallows to put in hot cocoa.
Robbie didn't want it. He thought hot things hurt his mouth.
He had tried to take a sip, but he just quickly spit it out!

Robbie stole some marshmallows, and Dede yelled out "Hey!"
Robbie only laughed at her and then he ran away.
"Soon it will be bedtime, so go off for now and play."
Then bedtime came and went and they began another day.

All week they tried to think of things to do,
but it was hard.

And sometimes Mama felt she couldn't wait
for school to start.

Usually most days they drove for hours in the car.

Sometimes she would drive 'til they could see
the moon and stars.

She said, "If Robbie is content
life's easier by far".

She knew her life and love
was in the rear view of her car.

She carried each one off to bed and
left their doors ajar.
Then softly whispered,

"I love you all,
just the way
you are."

Mom's Minute

In the beginning of the story Robbie smacks his head because he's upset. Self-injurious behavior like head banging and biting themselves is common when Autistic kids are upset. As Robbie got older, the week of Christmas break became increasingly difficult. He was bored staying home, yet he got upset when we went out anywhere. If we went out, he wanted to be home watching his movies. If we stayed home, he was bored watching the same movies over and over again. But if we tried to give him a new movie that he had never seen before, he refused to watch it! We were caught in this ridiculous cycle! He and I both couldn't wait for school to start up again so that he could go back to his routine.

Robbie hated wearing a hat or gloves and he would take them off in the car. The only way I could get him to keep his hat on was to put his hood on over the hat, and tie the strings under his chin. He couldn't get the string untied so it stayed on until I helped him untie it. We didn't sled very often but he did enjoy spending time with his sisters. The hardest thing was trying to find something to do during the winter.

Robbie did have a great sense of humor! When we went out to eat he would drink a sip of soda, and then he'd give you this look...and then he would blow raspberries! He cracked up laughing because he knew you would react! When he got older one of his aides thought he was spitting at her and I had to explain that he was playing with her and wanted her to laugh! Some Autistic kids don't understand sarcasm and don't really understand humor but they do want to make you laugh. So they will repeat something that they think may be funny because someone laughed at it before. But they may not have the best delivery of the joke. Some speak in "echolalia" meaning they repeat something that you just said. They may repeat movie lines repeatedly over and over again. It's because they don't really understand speech, but they do try to fit into our world and want to make us smile. Other times, it's because it's something that THEY enjoy, and they need to repeat it. I knew a girl once who repeated lines from Disney movies repeatedly and she called me Cinderella. Others repeat their daily activities over and over again. This is usually because they're stressed and they're trying to make sense of their world.

Sometimes playing outside worked, and sometimes it didn't! This day his boots came off and his feet were too cold!

The girls did their best to play with Robbie and keep him busy and happy out in the snow!

Here is Robbie looking through his videotape collection trying to decide what he wanted to watch. He was still watching the same movies at 27 years old.

CPSIA information can be obtained
at www.ICGtesting.com
Printed in the USA
BVHW051404220421
605637BV00012B/1735